PRAISE FOR
THE DEATH OF MOUNTAINS

"The Death of Mountains shifts the anthropocentric perspective
to tell a story not about our relationship to Nature, but Nature's
relationship to us. How small and temporary we are in the eyes of
a mountain, and yet how impactful in our beauty and ruthlessness.
This is a story to upset your idea of what it means to be a human, a
mountain, a death. It is a meditation on time and inevitabilities and
how one can stare pain in the face and still say yes; yes, it is all worth
it. I will never look at mountains the same way again."

K. Tidbeck,
author of *Amatka*

"As lyrical and rhythmic as bluegrass, grounded as the bones of
the Appalachians, ancient as stars and fresh as sunrise—Kurella
has written a sharp, tender tribute to the power of love and hope. I
would not have trusted this premise with anyone else."

Premee Mohamed,
author of *The Butcher of the Forest*

THE DEATH OF
MOUNTAINS

JORDAN KURELLA

ISBN: 978-1-59021-800-6

Front Cover and Interior by Inkspiral Design

Published by Lethe Press

*For my father and step-father,
who taught me to be wondrous
about the world.*

SUMMIT: PLUNDRED MOUNTAIN

On our hill, which is us, all things end. That is the way of things. We have seen this done over our crests and in our valleys. In the mines where people have scraped our walls for riches and died for worse. On our cliffs where lovers made their legacies and pushed others goodbye. We have seen the deaths of our sister mountains, and we have seen the Death of Mountains come for them. Sometimes, they were on time; sometimes they were late.

Now, they have come for us, and we will not have it. We have withstood death for far too long. Seen hundreds of our sisters felled by humanity and worse. We have seen people climb across our hillsides, die on them, kiss on them, feel things die inside us. We have heard so much birdsong, so much that we could not tell you all the songs' names (so many of the melodies are gone now). We are, in effect, history.

Little is left of history but the land and the scars people have left upon it.

When the Death of Mountains came for us, we had been aching for a long time. There is so much loss in being a mountain; it is a terribly long time to live. Yet something awoke within us when they arrived, their face a stone skull, their hands obsidian bones that cracked and crackled like fracking. It made us hurt to hear their earthquake step across the ground as they arrived. Their breath was like coal dust, the stuff their cloak was made from. They left a trail of oil behind them as they walked.

When they spoke, their breath was hot, volcanic; it made us wither at first. We, however, are a middling hill of the Appalachians. And we have seen much worse.

Far worse than death.

The Death of Mountains says, "Plundered Mountain, it's time to go."

And we say, "We are not ready, Death. We have too much yet to see."

The Death of Mountains smiles in fissures as they lower themselves to a felled branch with crackling knees. Their coal dust coat settles around them, painting the ground blighted.

"Tell me what's still so important that you still have to see it," they say.

"We can't know the future. No one can."

"I can." They reach out a hand. "Come on. It'll be a blast."

We sigh with a groan that we know comes from the people still inside us. Digging with their crude machines, with their thick words and hands thick with their toil. With their fatigue that hits harder and harder each day. Coated in the stuff Death of Mountains' cloak is made from.

"We can't. We can only tell you what we have seen, and why it is worth continuing. To see if it is worth seeing out. To see if it is worth waiting for."

Death of Mountains smile remains, as fissures tend to. "Waiting out? People? You know, as I do, that people are silly. No worse than insects. Worse than insects!"

"No," we say. "No."

"People are the ones who hurt you the most, who made you so hollow. Why do you even care?"

We would turn to Death of Mountains if we could, but we cannot. Our voice only mimics the idea of wistfulness, like a breeze across our trees. Our trees have seen better spring days than these. They've so little to hold on to, anymore. Our soil eroded, gone thin. It feeds no one any longer.

"It is also them who gives me the best memories."

"And the worst."

"What is joy without a little suffering?" we ask. "We can't have one without the other. It's not a life. It isn't."

"Speaking of life, yours has ended." The Death of Mountains stands. "Let's go."

"Have you had a little joy in your life, Death of Mountains?"

They pause. It's a trick we're playing, and they know it. Their hand hesitates before they drop it to their side, their slim shoulders slump as they look down my cliffside to the people exiting the mine for the day. The sunset slices through my gorge, lighting up the people's faces like daffodils.

"Guess I'm not killing you today, so I have time for stories." The Death of Mountains sits once more. "Stories, then. One from you and one from me, then the people will kill you tomorrow. It's gotta happen. I don't have time to sit here any longer than that."

Birds coo and settle in our delight.

"Very well," we say, "you go first. As our guest, it is only right and fair. A joyful story from the Death of Mountains, for us to hear. It will help ease us on our journey."

They seem amused by this. "You want a happy story? From me? Fine, sit and listen, and you'll get just that."

So, I do. And so, they begin.

THE DEATH OF MOUNTAINS' FIRST STORY

FOR THE SAKE OF THIS story, I am in Peru. I was in Peru, and it was raining in Peru for this story. Most expect that we Deaths enjoy the rains. But all Deaths are not the same; that is like saying all dogs are the same or all people are the same, but people and mountains and dogs know inherently that this is not true. I, Death of Mountains, do not like the rain. It makes climbing mountains and the job I have to do on them difficult. Which is not exactly killing, but not exactly not killing, either.

The rain was not pleasant. It was not the sort of drizzle that I could hardly feel on my bones. A rain that rushed the mud in rivers between my toe claws and sent rocks tumbling down the dying mountain face. It was a rain that might kill the mountain before I arrived to do it myself. And I was on my final warning regarding tardiness.

We Deaths are not the ones that do the actual killing. That is a fault in our branding; instead, we are more like chaperons or ushers or maître-d's. Of course, mountains might have no concept of these people-made things for people-type things. So, my job, as Death of Mountains, is to oversee a mountain's demise (each mountain's demise), the act and point of her death, ensure the death is recorded (the how and the why and the who by), and assure the mountain that they were (in fact) good.

All mountains are (in fact) good.

That last part is a joke, an attempt at humor, which I am (all told) terrible at as well. The point is this: Morality is outside of all Deaths' purview. We, as Deaths, simply take the soul of whatever Death we are assigned to and send it on its way. As Death of Mountains, I would take your soul and send your soul to wherever its meant to go. No, I don't know where that is. No, I don't know where it's going next or where you're meant to go. And no, I don't get to decide how you die.

That was decided by people far higher up, or lower down, than me.

Still, the fact remains that I am, all told, terrible at my job. I have been too often tardy, so many times I am far too late to kill so many mountains, as people had taken care of that for me. And far too early on killing others, as it was not yet their time. It is not an easy job being an entity of killing things so permanent that the very foundations of a landscape that people have in their heads are so unmovable and unshakable.

Yet here I am.

Plundered Mountain, you are one of the oldest mountains I have had the pleasure of killing, and you, being one of the Appalachians, remain one of the most stubborn. The Appalachians are the stubbornest range of mountains. So old and so proud, having stood on this earth longer than bones, longer than we Deaths have existed, you seem to think that you can outlast bones, that you can outlast us.

But all things die, even permanence. As a Death of permanent things, here I sit, and there I was, in Peru. For the sake of this story, I am climbing that particularly muddy mountain, falling down that particularly muddy mountain. I am scrambling up that mountain, likely to be late (again). I was there then, and it was the rainy season, and the rain was truly a deluge. The birdsong was nil, all other animals sheltered. Their noises and calls drowned out by the thunderous impact of raindrops on the soaked ground, and the likewise thunderous sound of a landslide screaming down the dying mountaintop.

Trees? There were nearly none, as people had taken them to make way for livestock and roads. People things for the benefit of the people themselves. Never for the mountain or the birds or the monkeys or the other things that lived here. Never for the benefit of humanity itself. People rarely see beyond the lifespan of their own nose. That is what the Death of People is for, and I'm getting lost in my story as I had gotten lost on that mountain.

I often get lost, it is why I am so terrible at so much.

As near as I was to the top, I could not see it. If I was indeed near to the top (and I was then). I knew that my handholds were as necessary as my footholds, and both were failing me as the stones I clung to slipped away as easily as thinking. The mountain, however, knew I was coming. She must have. As when I reached the top— the summit, her summit—I stood on that peak and looked out at all the other mountains. Mountains less taken for their trees and resources. Far less shallow in height and less easy to pass over and dig caverns through as she was?

She sighed.

"Are you here for us, Death of Mountains?" she asked. "We are Colina Cansada."

She had been waiting for me for days, and the rains had never calmed. She was full of sighs, sending more trees tumbling down her hillside roots over crest. The death of a mountain brings destruction not only to the mountain itself, but all life upon it, and sometimes below it, and around it. It is quite the to-do. This is something I understand, being what I am. It is something mountains understand, being who you are. It is something very few beyond you or I understand, being who they are. A tree or a rabbit or a person cannot understand the vastness of a mountain, the idea of a loss of such an ecosystem. That you are indeed a house and a home to so many, a place of work, and a place of thought. A landmark, and a stop-gap. That when I come for you, or you die, so much goes with you.

That I, myself, am the first to arrive, and then other Deaths follow swiftly. Yet again I am lost in my story as I had gotten lost climbing Colina Cansada, as I will likely lose my job. As I have been lost so many times before. For the sake of this story, Colina Cansada is talking to me, and she, unlike you, Plundered Mountain, is begging to die. She, unlike you, is in horrible pain, and has been for some time. For the sake of this story, I was in Peru, and Colina Cansada had far fewer trees than you.

So much had been taken from her: her life, her soil, her minerals, her happiness. Like you, she had been cleaved into, bored into, mined, and stolen from. But she, unlike you, was far less magnificent, and in far more of a state of despair.

For the sake of this story, Colina Cansada said,

"Death of Mountains, we are dying. Please do us the honor."

"Yes," I said, solemnly and importantly.

As I can be, sometimes, solemn and important.

"We are waiting."

Upon the street below and deep within her, I heard the machines still going. Their sounds screeching and keening over the steady pound of the rain. Delving, cutting, drilling. The felling of trees and the cracking of rock only added to the sighs of Colina Cansada, and every sigh was another landslide. Every flinch another rockslide. She was so close to death; in placing my hand upon her I could feel the tremblings of her last hanging on. The vibrations of the machines rattling up through what was left of her meager mountain bones.

"How much longer do you have, Colina Cansada?" I asked.

"A day, perhaps half again. They mean to cleave us in two, to make way for more of their machines so they may cut down more mountains, to give you more to do."

This was many, many years ago; I was busy then, with no idea how busy I'd become.

"Right, I will kill you. But I want to do something else your passing."

"Something else?" Her voice was so tired and tiring more through the effort of speaking.

"These damn people need to understand what you are. All of them: the men, the women, the others. Every single one."

She sighed once again. "If it takes you longer to do this, don't. Get it over with."

Her sighs turned to labored breaths as the people continued to labor and cut and cleave and bore into her sides to cleave the mountain in twain. To ensure that she made safe passage for their machines and whatever other horrid things industry had in mind for the next mountain, and the next mountain, and the next. Her breaths were in tandem with the speed of the machines, quick quick slow. Quick quick slow. The heart of the mountain a thundering thing. It made my own heart do the same.

What did this mean for her, for all mountains. For all that lived upon them. What did this mean for my work? Still the rains went on, still the machines went on. I could not. There was a time and a place to send a mountain on, and it was not when people were there to see it. Such spectacle as I was planning was not fit for them. So, I waited as Colina Cansada continued to slip away.

My waiting was rewarded, fortuitously, as the people left the mountain held together by rods and poles, her weight impossibly unsupported with all their machines huddled inside, sheltered from the evening rains by tarps and twine. They left, wheels spinning away in their vehicles that spouted smoke that resembled my cloak. This, they did not know, was poor placement.

And still I waited.

The rains became as thick as the day's heat, and it was then that I climbed to Colina Cansada's peak, and I did my work. Her demise was beautiful in its atrocity. I placed my staff in the tip of what was left of her peak, and I brought it down low, wrapping my stone claws around it. Lower and lower it went, delving down into Colina Cansada's tired earth. Her dying earth, and that earth collapsed in upon itself, the staff sending it to its next place, where she could be a dog, perhaps. Or maybe a person. Or a star.

In her collapse, she fell over and over upon herself. A landslide upon landslides. Collecting rocks, and what was left of her trees. She consumed her own caves and filled them with what was left of her earth. All told, I did a very good job, as this mass of mountain—this mass of dead mountain—held up by poles and rods, which had once sheltered expensive and shrieking machines, destroyed them all. Destroyed all the machines with a blow so crushing the metal sang out for a moment before it was silent forevermore.

Her last sigh was a thank you, I decided. Though it likely wasn't.

In killing this particular mountain, I did so with silly hope. The hope was that people wouldn't try these tricks again. I was naïve: having seen these machines do this so many times, I thought, maybe one disaster would make people think twice. Three times, if I was lucky. How naïve I was so many years ago.

Colina Cansada had become blissfully an ex-mountain. She has been sent elsewhere, and is likely joyful, showing the rest that she could enact revenge on those who mistreated her so, as a star, or a person, or a dog.

This is what I wish for you, dear Plundered Mountain.

SUMMIT'S REFRAIN: PLUNDERED MOUNTAIN

ON OUR HILL, WHICH IS US, Death of Mountains finishes their story when it is still nighttime, and the moon is rising. We are already collecting the early spring dew that cools us and makes us chill with the story of this other mountain's final triumph. We delight in Death of Mountains' kindness in allowing Colina Cansada her final victory.

Yet we have questions.

Something so old as mountains, and something so old as death, always has questions. Questions are sometimes seen by people as something for the innocent and the aged: that asking about a thing is so infantile, that knowing (or pretending to know) is a sign of maturity and focus. However, we beings of immutable eternity, we mountains and the Deaths, know that questions themselves provide answers.

And we know that answers themselves, and more to that—the giving of the answers—tell more than knowing (or pretending to know) ever could.

While we have questions, we do not want to ask them yet. Asking questions now would not delay the Death of Mountains in the act they have come to do. They have already admitted their penchant and problem for tardiness. Which is one of our questions. The other of our questions is how, in fact, does something so permanent die. How does one reconcile with being a Death of such permanent things?

We can see the task of this permanence weighs upon Death of Mountains with how their entire body hunches over; how they lean upon their staff as if they are put upon by time itself. Time has been kind to us, my sisters and us, ourselves. We have lived and experienced many things, many joyful, many painful. Yet we have seen much and loved more. Death of Mountains only erases all that love and joy and experience.

The things we would wish to ask them would only weigh upon them more: How could they, in all their understanding of how they work, take away so much life at the request of something that does not understand it?

Still, we do not ask. We do not think we ever will. Instead, we will tell a story, as it is our turn.

Death of Mountains sits on their log, which creaks under them, as weak as the tree was when it fell, and as heavy as Death of Mountains' bones are, being made from stone. They wait for us, as the bargain we struck said they would. As they had promised.

"Shall we tell our story now?" we ask.

As it is only polite to ask.

"Go ahead," they say, their face looking up to the moon. "We have all night. I can't kill you until the workers return in the morning, otherwise it looks suspicious."

"Isn't dying often unpredictable? Why can't it look suspicious."

The Death of Mountains does not turn their face back to us as they speak. "Unpredictable isn't the plan I had in mind."

"Must a plan always be followed?"

Now their gaze turns back to us slowly, taking their time. The moon creaks through the sky as their bones creak and crackle like fractures. We would be concerned, but our concern has long since passed. There is only so much concern we can hold when we are holding death on our shoulder.

"Just gimme this one thing, Plundered Mountain, okay? This one thing. I already have had so much taken away from me already."

The tone with which the Death of Mountains speaks is so melancholy. Such a quiet warning of a coming avalanche of emotion that we bother them no further. The questions we plan to ask will come, but we will wait. And we are exceptionally good at waiting.

"Let us tell our story, then."

THE PLUNDERED MOUNTAIN'S FIRST STORY

PEOPLE BEGIN THEIR STORIES WITH *Once upon a time*, but we mountains are different. Time is not something we count like people do, as it is a different entity for us than it is for people. It marks us differently, is less important. Mountains do not have beginnings, only endings. So, we begin our stories like this:

On our hill, which is us, there was once a cave. This cave was once very small and housed people and animals from storms. It also housed things people wanted that could fuel things people wanted, they would discover as more people came to live within view of the top of the hill which was us.

It was in this way that the cave grew from a small mouth to a deep and diving thing.

But this is not a story about a cave, nor is it a

story about us. This is a story about a bird, and a man who could sing like it. It is a rule codified by deep and diving men that every hill like us must have a canary. A small yellow bird in a cage which whistles a particular call all day long within our cavernous underbelly.

It was the habit of this man, whose arms stretched to his knees and whose shoulders held back the morning and rolled forward the night, to whistle like the canary. This was much to the dismay of his friends. We say this man enjoyed his friends in the way that a mountain might say we enjoyed having deep and diving caves. This man did not enjoy his friends; he did not enjoy his work; and he did not enjoy the deep and diving confines of the cave.

What he enjoyed was tending to the canary.

It is the habit of all mountains to know what goes on upon our hills, and within our walls. Within our caves and in our deep and diving mines. When someone picks a flower, we rejoice at their wonder at what they have found. When they kiss their lover under a tree, we delight in the lover's delight also. We feel the sorrow of the lovers who wander our hills searching for loneliness. And we feel the strikes of the pickaxes and the machines that core out our centers.

We also hear the conversations between canary and man.

So it was to this end that we listened to the conversations between this particular canary, and this particular man. This man had a name, but it is not important to us, as names are not. However, the canary's name was Sunshine, which is important to us, as the sun shining is important to us. The canary's name hit us with the same hurt as a pickaxe strike: bold and unnerving, as this canary rarely knew the feel of the sun upon his feathers. He rarely saw the light of day. He did not know the cant of the sun across the sky, or the shadows it threw across our canyons.

Yet that was his name, and it remains important to us.

The man whistled a song about sunshine to him and taught it to him. Sunshine could not repeat it back, of course. Not like other birds could mimic such things, like the crow can. It wasn't that Sunshine wasn't clever, he was plenty clever. It was simply that Sunshine wasn't that sort of bird. And birds are as different as mountains and are as different as flowers: they are meant to sing different songs and meant to do different tasks. It was Sunshine's particular task to alert the men in the deep and diving cave that they were all about to die.

It was his only friend's particular task to ensure he was fed. That he had water. And lastly, that he was alive and what he was singing at all. Of course, we know from the beginning of this tale how it will end, or we think it will. Every story does that: fools someone into believing how it will go.

So, the man whose shoulders held back the morning whistled to the canary all day long for many sunups and sunsets. And each day, he whistled to him on his way out. Some days he took Sunshine with him, arriving last out of the cave mouth, alone on the elevator, and walking down the canyon path, both whistling and singing together.

The next day, he would arrive once again before the sun had yet arrived and take the elevator down with Sunshine in his hand. He was happiest when the two of them were together. Feathers alight and bright, Sunshine grew fat and beautiful voiced on all the man's attentions.

It is a truth that all things in nature that are fat are happy.

On the day one would expect the ending of this story to happen, it happened when the man whose shoulders held back the morning had taken Sunshine home with him. He brought Sunshine down the elevator all alone, and ensured he was fed. Ensured he had water, and whistled along with him as he walked along the corridors, lighting lanterns, righting signs.

As he did, he noticed when he did not answer. So, he whistled the tune again. And again, Sunshine did not answer. His song was absent in the cave, and the man paused in lighting the next torch, rushing back through the dark to the canary cage. The lights extinguished in the man's wake, the signs bent and bowed to him. He undid everything he had done as he whistled Sunshine's song back to no one.

And the bird did not answer.

The elevator rumbled its descent, scraping along the walls with the chatter of false friends. Creaking and cracking of the wood under the scuff of work boots, and the man whose shoulders rolled forward the night was at Sunshine's cage. And Sunshine was gone. The deep and diving cave was no longer safe. Nothing was safe. Not Sunshine, not him, not the others coming to take what we had kept safely inside ourselves for so long.

Yet no one is a martyr, there is no such thing, we have learned in our eternity in this place. Watching the people upon our hillsides crying and wishing for death. We have shown them such beauty with the turn of a tree leaf, with a gentle push of our moss to show them a violet, or a lucky clover. No one will remember one man's sacrifice for a canary he loved. Even if he did mean the world to him.

When the elevator touched upon surface floor, the one these people had dug out with their clawing machines and their rumbling tools, the man whose shoulders rolled forward the night did not unchain the door. Instead, he held up the small body of Sunshine. Cooling and not yet stiff in his hands. His friends inside undid the door and let him in as he cradled the dead bird to his chest to keep him warm.

The ascent was long, but to the man whose shoulders rolled forward the night, it was not long enough. We watched him walk alone from the cave mouth as his friends walked ahead, smiling and carrying on, leaving him behind. He stumbled as he walked. His footsteps scraping the ground, stuttering on the silt and dirt of the canyon floor. His body cast a long shadow like a statue in the dawn light, his shoulders so broad. His long arms cradling his friend. We could see his sorrow tattooed on the ground before each step, and we knew.

We knew what a thing it was to save so many lives at the cost of a favorite.

SUMMIT'S REFRAIN: PLUNDERED MOUNTAIN

ON OUR HILL, WHICH IS US, Death of Mountains turns their face down from the moon to look at our peak as we finish our story. It was a story that neither answered any questions we had for them nor did it pose any further questions, but perhaps it would cause them to think about what exactly they were doing. Their face showed no evidence that the story had moved them, yet their shoulders rose and fell with a steady motion.

We took a breath, shaking off the dew from tree leaves and moss and clover into our soil. It rolled down the hill into the canyons and into the rivulets and into rabbit warrens and fox holes and deer thickets. The Death of Mountains shook the dew from their bone hands with a single motion, and stood, the cracking of their bones once again like fracking. Damp in this way, they smelled of petrichor.

They gave every evidence that they wanted to be alone upon my peak. Which is where most people come when they want to be alone. We wonder if Death of Mountains knows how human they are in this way. We do not know if they understand how much they are, indeed, like people, the very beings they had claimed to be worse than insects.

When they open their eyes, slowly at first, then quickly as a sinkhole forming—as dark and as mesmerizing—they smile at me, sadly. "Have you met Death of People?" they ask. "I've had the displeasure of meeting him a couple of times. He is his own Death, nearly a person himself. But I think that comes with the territory."

"No, we have never met Death of People. Seen him, yes, many times, in many of his guises, but always he stays away from us properly. Never starts conversation." We watch Death of Mountains' grip change on their staff three times, either in annoyance or processing the information. "We do find it clever that you Deaths resemble your work. You, by example, resemble a mountain."

They nearly ignore our last comment, their gaze fixed on the ground, but I hear the smile in their voice when they respond. "He's afraid of permanent things, unlike me. That's why he changes. I can stay this way forever as fashion doesn't bother me."

They shift on the log, setting their legs more steady (more permanent) on the moss.

"Yet you and I know, Death of Mountains, that permanence is a lie."

"Yeah, I know that. I know that, and you know that. But him? He's a lot smarter than he looks." They look off to the side. "By which I mean, he's not very smart."

Death of Mountains laughs, then. A breath of a laugh, it whistles from their crag of a mouth, like geyser steam. As gently as the laugh left them, the laugh falls to silence along with our own silence to the moss below, and we regard them as they return their posture to stone. All of Death of Mountains runs hot and cold, like the earth itself, constantly in motion, in flux, a source of immutable fury and friction. It is no wonder they are always frustrated. To be so alive and yet to have no life of your own.

They are as stoic as a mountain, yet as emotional as the wind.

THE DEATH OF PEOPLE'S FIRST STORY

GOT A STORY FOR YOU, and it goes like this: being everywhere at once used to be easier. Way easier. There was a time—before were swords, before metal at all—when my job was chill. Someone would kill someone else with their hands (or maybe a rock), and that took fucking conviction. A person really had to *think* about killing someone back in the day. Wars were so much harder to fight. But no, people are incredibly inventive, which is the most annoying thing about them.

Their ingenuity is what makes my job super difficult.

It's not that I hate people; I hate the things they've built: swords, guns (I really hate guns), tanks, bombs. I hate their bigger bombs, and bigger tanks, and even bigger-er guns. They're inventive at coming up with ways of killing one another off. A lot of stuff people have invented have put the other Deaths on my ass, cause their inventions end up killing off everything else. This ends up being somehow my fault. Like I have any kind of control over people's need to create shit.

So here I am in another-er war zone, right? Everything is rubble. Don't know if I'm standing in a road or a school or a hospital or a grocery store right now, but I do know that I am standing in a bunch of work. A bunch of work created by people because other people wanted to destroy people they didn't like. It's way more complicated than that, but I don't get bogged down in the details. Details are not in my purview.

My job isn't to judge where souls go. I don't know—or care—whether people were good or bad. What their life was like. What they did or who they were. That's not my position or what I'm supposed to get involved in. My job is to pick them up and send them along their way, all aspects of me, everywhere at once. So, while I'm in this war zone, I am also at a grocery store, at a school, at a hospital bed, in a person's bathroom. And so on and so on and so on.

But this story I got right now is this war zone, and I've picked up and sent along probably thirty souls? Forty? Lost count around twenty-three. So many were kids. There were so many children's hands I picked up and sent along the way, with bewildered eyes, of not knowing how they ended up this way or why they ended up this way, and it would be heartbreaking if I had a heart. But it's enough to make me want to quit.

I've tried to quit, but I am, all told, way too good at my job.

So, it's the thirty-seventh soul or the forty-eighth, I can't remember (like I said), and a hand, a real human hand, comes up and touches me on my back, grabbing onto my jacket. I feel it the way I feel anything in this world. The wind, the sun on my face, anything that's real and wonderful. Or anything that's real and horrible.

This hand is wonderful in the fact that it's real and horrible because I know (probably) that anything I have to say isn't going to go well. The person is leaning on me heavily. I can tell before I even turn that they're tired, more tired than me. That they're tired of all of this. We're both standing on uneven rubble, and our emotions are equally unstable.

I turn my head slowly and as people-ly as I can.

"Hello," I say, in the language of this place.

"Hello," the person says back. "Do you have any water? Food? Anything. I am so hungry and so tired."

They do look tired and uninjured. But this is not a place for both those things to hang out at the same time. It's way too open and way too sunny, and this person's shadow is long, and they make a helluva great target for, well, anything really. Since I can't die cause I am a Death, nothing can hit me or target me. A perk, really.

But also, since they can see me, I know they don't have long. Also, though, since they can see me, I start caring about them because I am a dumb son of a whatever that has my empathy jacked as high as it can go.

"Sorry," I say. "I don't have any water. But if you follow me, I'll take you to some shelter."

I really do know where there's shelter. I do, or I did. Dunno if it's there now, and don't really care. All I really care about is that this person has a good life for the last few minutes, hours, or half a day that they can. That is in my purview. And while the other aspects of me move on from here to there and everywhere else, this aspect of me (this me of me telling this story) is keeping this person's story alive by telling it here.

Their name was Mahamoud, and they used to run a newsagent a few kilometers north. They sold magazines and newspapers, but they also sold water and sodas and their favorite thing to sell was energy drinks.

"I drank too many of those; my doctor was always saying that if I kept it up, my heart would just stop one day. Stop, like a watch. I wish it had, you know, just stopped. Stopped before all this shit. If my doctor had ever been right about all the bad things I did: the energy drinks, the smoking, the sweets, I would have missed all of this."

"Doctors mean well, but they don't got all the answers."

"Does anyone have all the answers?"

"You'd be surprised, Mahamoud. You'd be surprised."

"So, no one does." They smile then and sit down on what used to be, well, something, who knows, underneath a precariously perched upper floor of, well, something else. They slowly lower themselves with popping knees and the telltale aches and pains of a person who has worked too long and hard their entire life.

I smile at them, and they smile back.

"Thanks," they say. "I never got your name."

"You don't need it," I say, and I extend my hand, and Mahamoud's soul gently exits their tired and aching body and comes along with me.

Sometimes, I really love my job. Love it so much I need a day off. The job hurts, not like Mahamoud's knees or their back. Not like a gunshot or a railing to the head or something like that or anything. Just seeing a smile on the face before death or a family crowded around a hospital bed. That shit really hurts.

Death of People, however, doesn't get days off.

SUMMIT'S REFRAIN: PLUNDERED MOUNTAIN

On our hill, which is us, back upon the precipice of the cliff that divides me in two, the Death of Mountains turns once again to face the moon. It is higher in the sky now, but only barely. This is how we mark the passage of time: moon, stars, sun. But the stars have winked out many by many over the years. So few are in the sky now as the city gets closer to us.

The Death of Mountains has been silent for some time after rising slowly from their log to walk to the edge of me to see what people have wrought. To see what they have done to make me fit their needs. The highway that cut away part of me once was new, and people drove along it quickly with motorcycles as a novelty then. Over time, people used it as they used all things: out of necessity and habit.

Roads, the link between two places, remain useful only as a means to an end.

We are watching the Death of Mountains as the road remains silent for a while as they do. Standing still as statues, their cloak billowing coal dust down to my moss-covered floor. The moss has been dying for some time. We have been dying for some time, yet we have so much we want to see. The people in the mines, we care about them. The deer have new fawns, and always will. The rabbits in their warrens, the bears are soon to emerge from hibernation.

Life must continue, and so must we.

"Your story was sad," they say. "How many more of those do you have in you?"

"Endless stories," we say. "We can tell stories forever."

"I can't hear you talk forever; it's exhausting."

"Perhaps instead of telling stories for a moment, we play a game," we say.

"What kind of game?" they ask, turning back to look at us.

"A game where we ask you a question, and then you ask us a question."

"That's not a game! That's a conversation."

They sound both annoyed and amused. As if we are the child and they are the permanent entity. Yet without us, they would not exist. So, who is the child? They do not realize they are the one being petulant.

"The game is," we say, our voice rumbling and low like a rockslide, "that you must always and only tell the truth in your answers."

The Death of Mountains' shoulders fall, and they lean on their stone staff. They are exhausted with us: with our playfulness, with our stories, with our delay upon delay upon delay. They stare once again below, down at the forgotten highway. As all things, we know when someone is upon us, or what used to be us. The highway is part of us, and we can see it: a lone car driving down the road with a single headlight. Driving quickly, packed full of suitcases and clothes. Quickly done, with the driver leaning close to the wheel, staring and gripping tight. Death of Mountains also sees this, and we both watch the tiny car until its taillights fade from view.

They are curious. We have seen this scene a thousand times.

"You speak in riddles, Plundered Mountain."

"We do not; you're only stalling because you do not want to play."

They turn and look at us, still petulant, still a child. "Fine, I will play your game of questions. Who goes first?"

We are happy, our voice filled with joy when we say, "It is only fair that you begin, Death of Mountains, as we told the last story. The first question is yours."

They turn to our peak, their fissured grin eking across their face.

"Fine then," they say, "I'll begin."

THE FIRST GAME OF QUESTIONS

Death of Mountains: "For my first question, I will ask: Why don't you want to die?"

Plundered Mountain: "We think it a very normal thing, to not want to die. Most people avoid it, most animals avoid it, most beings in general avoid it. The only things that do not avoid it are the machines people build. Those are excellent at dying and not dying.

Why should it be customary for a living thing to want to die when there is so much yet in the world to see? To wonder about? The vehicle you watched driving down the road with its single headlight. Where was the driver going at such a late hour, with their car packed with things? They drove so quickly and so fast. Were they driving to something or away from something? We cannot help but wonder about such small things as this and still wonder at the larger things, such as where the stars have gone. There used to be so many, and now there are so few. The birds are the same: on our hill, which was us, there were once several different kinds of birdsong. Now, we can recognize all the birds that come to sit in our tree branches.

We know all the songs; we can name them.

So, we wonder, what happens to our earth, should we go. Does it fall with the rest of us? To the deep and diving depths? Or are we to be left shattered and sundered to never wonder at these things alone?"

The Death of Mountains: "You cheated. For my second question, I ask: Why should you care?"

Plundered Mountain: "'Is it not in the nature of all shoulders to hold up the cares that weigh upon them?' We heard a poet say that about us once when trying to write about the nature of mountains while looking over our cliffs, when we had more trees and when the stars were more plentiful.

At least, we assumed him a poet. Who else should speak that way? In such a lonely manner, all by himself with such dark clothing and ill-suited shoes for a walk?

If we, as a mountain, are not shoulders to hold up the cares and lives of what lives upon and within our caves and our eddies and our ravines and so forth, then what are we? We hold up the cares, so in turn, we care. It is the reciprocal nature of nature itself: to give and, in return, to give back. That is what people took from us. That is what people took. Not all people, of course. The poet, for one, we do not know his full life, but he gave to us, and so we give to you, Death of Mountains, his thoughts. The people who scrape our insides and dive deep within us, they take. Those who remove our trees and cut us in twain to build the road you watched the car drive between so quickly? It is not the driver's fault; they do not think of how we used to be, only where they are going. Or perhaps where they came from.

It is the fault of people. The people who came and the people who will arrive in the morning. Still, the fault does not lie with them. Many of them need only to do the work, many of them are bidden only to do the work. It is not entirely people but the work of few. Most pain put upon the land comes at the hands of a few."

The Death of Mountains: "So why not release yourself from that pain?"

Plundered Mountain: "It is not in the nature of us to falter. We are a middling hill in the Appalachians. We do not give up. We do not relent under hardship. We have seen five hundred mountains fall under the hands of machines and the people who control them. We will not be a casualty of this.

It is our turn at a question."

Plundered Mountain: "Why are you so consistently late?"

The Death of Mountains: "It's not my fault. People do such a terrific job of doing my job that I arrive too late to do my own job. It's like traffic, right? Always there and still always in the way. Somehow it manages to make even the most well-meaning person incredibly late for something they mean to be on time for. Regardless of whatever or whenever. It's infuriating, frankly. I'm incensed."

Plundered Mountain: "If people do your job so well, why not quit?"

The Death of Mountains: "This is a question I constantly ask myself as I climb another mountain that is dying, or in pain, or like you, simply will not face the fact that it is time, and she stalls. You all stall, do you not realize? The ones of you that have pending Death—making me late once again, not only for your death but the death of several other mountains. So here I sit, with you, in this ridiculous game of yours, as a respite. Even though I know it will make me late for another death, either one caused by people or a similarly stubborn hill like you."

Plundered Mountain: "There is nothing so stubborn as a mountain."

The Death of Mountains: "That's not a question. Game over."

SUMMIT'S REFRAIN: PLUNDERED MOUNTAIN

ON OUR HILL, WHICH IS US, the Death of Mountains returns to their log as the moon travels overhead. Waxing and looming above as another stubborn beacon of what yet remains: so few stars, but the moon will never give up. As the stars on our hill, which is us, we have seen stars so plentiful that the deer could not sleep in their rutting season and fought on two legs all the night long when the moon was full.

When the moon was full winters and winters ago, the stars lit up the night bright as daylight, and there was near to no difference. And now, on nights like tonight, when the moon waxes toward that direction (fullness) the person in the car driving to or from something with a single headlight? Where they lean so close to the steering wheel that we wonder if they can see properly at all.

That was both a long time ago and tonight. We are delaying time. We are making Death of Mountains angry. However, we have learned they are tired; we have learned they are tired with their job. They have learned we are not tired with being a mountain. There must be something we can do about our joint predicament. Something to benefit us all.

"If you do not mind, Death of Mountains, I would ask another question."

They sigh with breath like coal dust, falling heavy in the cold April air. It catches on the breeze and hits the ground some ways away from them but does not blacken it. The oil slick of their feet pools but does not collect, as their breath does not collect. They have come to collect one thing, and we will not allow them to take it.

"The game is over, but fine. Go ahead."

"What would make you happy at the end of this encounter?"

"For the job to be done. For my job here, specifically, to be done."

We pause. A pause nearly as full as the moon and with a thought nearly as bright. The thought of finality makes us shiver, upsetting a rabbit from her warren. She runs out, sees the Death of Mountains, and they move politely out of the way to let her pass. With this thought, we know that we might (potentially, perhaps) be on the right path.

"Those are three separate roads to happiness, you understand," we say. "Three separate outcomes."

"How do you figure?"

"In the first outcome, I die. Yes. Yet perhaps not by your hand." We pause a moment; there is a sound in the underbrush: A bear is waking from her hibernation. She will sense Death is near and be skittish. She will feel the rumbles of my speaking and be skittish. But we, ourselves, have nothing to fear. "The second outcome, the job is done. By which you have killed me. Well done, you."

"And the third?"

"The third, something else entirely." We pause as the bear pauses; it senses that something is different. Something is amiss. "We would like you to tell us another story. The night is far from over, and we have so much time to go before we die."

"Less than you think," they say. "But fine."

And they begin.

THE DEATH OF MOUNTAINS' SECOND STORY

FOR THE SAKE OF THIS story, I am very close to losing my job.

There are only so many times a Death can be late for their appointed killing. One too many times, fault applied or not, and that Death meets reprimand. There is no killing a Death, but sanctions are applied. Sanctions have been applied across several deaths for several decades, and no matter how much we Deaths have complained to Below, no one there seems to understand that times now are not how times used to be.

Things are on fast forward, and we can't keep up.

The first sanction, I lost my ability to travel quickly, this was a terrible idea and was reversed just as quickly as it was put in place. It only made me later and later and later to several other killings, and Below realized that they didn't have enough sanctions on hand to keep up with the amount of tardies on my record. So, they took that away and applied this instead: I became small.

Once, I was as tall as a mountain. I loomed giant and imposing, could speak to a peak on her own level. Look at her height with my own. Now, I am approximately as tall or as short as an average person (give or take an average). This makes me about as imposing as nothing at all, being far shorter than a tree or even most bears. To a mountain, this is nothing. I have only my appearance to guide my station. How am I meant to guide a mountain along to her resting place without looking her in the eye?

Now I scramble up her sides like any other person, rather than appear at a mountain's side. It's embarrassing. And this makes me later, too, but Below won't hear my complaints. They say I complain too much. They say that Death of Rivers doesn't complain nearly this much.

They do, they're simply too fed up to follow through.

The second sanction for my tardiness, which happened in the last five years, was that I could not simply usher a mountain along. This has only, once again, increased my instances of lateness, and made Below even more upset with me. Those in power do not seem to understand that being the size I am, and not being able to usher mountains onward create a lack of confidence to get things done. Not my confidence, but anyone else's. The other Deaths don't think I can do it, mountains don't think I can do it, soon I'm going to start believing it myself.

As I'm no longer imposing, and now I have to bargain with mountains in order to kill them, existence is extremely tedious. Mountains are the stubbornest things on Earth. Perhaps second only to plague. But plague is Death of People's problem, and we won't get into that. He understands people better than anyone; and yet still gets weirded out by them. Which is normal.

And so, my lateness compounds and compounds until my third and final sanction will arrive, which is this: I will receive a promotion. A promotion to work where I will be demoted to work as an operator in Below, and not be a Death at all. This is the final and most humiliating sanction (being promoted). To unmake a Death is to unmake our entire purpose and will. This is, perhaps, why Below does what it does: to unmake us. We don't unmake anything, that's a misnomer in our titles, but in unmaking us, it's a final irony in what we're perceived to be.

When there is nothing before me but my final sanction and a life in Below deciding the fate of other Deaths and their temporary turmoil upon this changing earth, the third option: *what could stop a*

Death from being a Death other than being completely unmade? The answer is sanctions, the answer is Below. The fact is that should I even walk away from all of this (to cease being a Death at all), I will still be found. How am I, being as I am, looking as I am, meant to do (to be) anything else?

I've never been anything else.

Can an entity such as a Death become anything but themselves? Can I, Death of Mountains, change my very being into something other than my intended purpose? Over my years of walking and ushering, I have heard so many stories: of so many people's lives, animals' lives, trees' lives. Mountains have told me of what they have seen, and I, in turn have traded very little of myself in return.

However, you, Plundered Mountain, have turned my time on its end, near The End. Closing in on what is to be my third sanction, when a new Death of Mountains will probably be appointed. But that's the thing, isn't it? I'm not the problem, Below is the problem, people are the problem. Why do I need to walk away from being an entity when I haven't done anything wrong? Not really.

Maybe I'm not cut out to do this. Maybe I'm not the one who's as smart as they look.

SUMMIT'S REFRAIN: PLUNDERED MOUNTAIN

ON OUR HILL, WHICH IS US, we listen to Death of Mountains' second story. There is something rumbling underneath their story, something moving and living. Something hidden and sacred. As a mountain, I understand this. It speaks thicker and richer and with roots deeper than they can see or believe in. The thread that rings through their story, weaving in and out like whispers is this: Death of Mountains is most afraid of what they cannot control.

What they cannot control is how death occurs, and how it occurs is most often at the hands of people and their machines. Mountains, such as us, such as my sisters, once stood as monuments of grace and prayer and worship. Things of wonder and sometimes destruction (a volcano is, truly, an angrier and more conversant mountain). So, when Death of Mountains speaks, they do not understand the core of their hopes, the core of their worries is this.

It is death itself: death at the hands of people, and their machines.

Dying is neither graceful nor peaceful for so many. Those that do die peacefully and gracefully are so few that they are the subject of fictions and songs that I hear people tell of lovers and mothers. Those that loved them stand upon my hills and rewrite their history with the hitch of lies in their voice.

Death of Mountains' stony face, a skull made of rock with caves for eyes, and a crag for a mouth, is tilted toward our peak, and we witness in their shoulders and how they hold their staff how tired they are. They are tired of being small; they are done with bargaining. They want solutions, this Death of Mountains who can find only problems, so they may end them.

"What would you have us do? Change the way of things?"

Their shoulders fall slightly more, akin to sighing, but without the effort of it.

"I didn't ask that," they say, turning their head toward the gorge where the miners will arrive to kill us in the morning. "It's just a possibility. An exhausting possibility, but it's one I never considered. Did you ever consider being anything but a mountain?"

"We are everything *and* a mountain, Death of Mountains."

"How do you figure?"

It is our turn to sigh, and we sigh happily, sending more dew running to the thickets and the burrows and the rivers. "We are a mountain, yes. But we are also a home to rivers, to foxes, to deer. A home to so many insects and flowers and trees that we cannot name them all. We are home to spiders and clover. We are a home to ideas and kisses and engagements and murder. We are a home to resources and roads and—"

The Death of Mountains stands, quickly this time.

"I get it," they say, standing to loom over the mining gorge. "It's your turn for a story, Plundered Mountain. The people will be here in the morning, and I haven't decided yet whether to let them kill you or not. Convince me, one way or the other."

They have said it, but our game began when they set foot at our peak. We have been trying to convince them of this decision since our first story, but perhaps Death of Mountains could not see it. In our time with them, we learned that entities such as Deaths perceive all things with immediacy; yet we mountains see time as eternal, decisions as lingering, all things as being a long time until their end.

A plan can become a plan before it ever has a reason to be set in motion.

To this end, we begin our second story.

THE PLUNDERED MOUNTAIN'S SECOND STORY

ON OUR HILL, WHICH IS US, there lived a pair of mourning doves. They were to be in love forever as mourning doves are betrothed to be, the silly things, as forever is a terribly long time, and persists both before and after death. But that idea is beyond the scope of all things, including birds. So, these mourning doves were quite in love, which is the strongest of all emotions. It lifts as much as it breaks; kills as much as it heals.

Love is a devastating thing, so we mountains do not meddle in it.

The mourning doves had several years to make several nests, and for the length of many summers and many winters, their calls could be heard the length of my rivers and gorges. From tree to tree they flew, always together, never apart. Yet, there is a reason they are called mourning doves, is there not?

One would think that is what this story is about, but it isn't. Scaling the scope of this story, the way a man scales my hills, one would think that a hawk is to fly down and take one of the pair in her talons away. Leaving the other lonely and alone, forever crying out for the other. To remain before and after death as a widow or widower.

Yet that would be placing the end before the beginning.

The mourning doves of this story were always together, betrothed to be that way. As two, never more, until they came upon another, much younger dove of the same. A lone mourning dove, who had likely stumbled upon the fate mentioned earlier. The one with the hawk, or the eagle, or some other such bird of prey. Perhaps a machine or a person. The details here are unimportant.

As people who once studied nature wrote in their dusty books over and over: there are always only two: a boy and a girl. Never different, never wavering. Never three, never more. Never a girl and a girl. Never a boy and a boy. Damn the frogs who change gender at a whim even when there is no sense on it. Damn the anomalies, as they must be so. Yet we know, being a mountain, that the only law nature follows is cruelty (as people see it), but we see it as what it is: life.

The mourning doves did what people who study nature once deemed impossible, yet nature does not play by the laws of dusty dead people who wrote dusty old books. The doves took some time getting acquainted: making themselves look magnificent, preening one another, flitting about the branches and repeating the same. They did this until the sun was set and it was settled, the betrothed two became three.

The three became many more. They made a nest, they had squabs and raised them, the squabs took flight, and the three remained together, much to the disagreement of any book that might otherwise say so. People came and watched the birds, and they commented how one dove always tailed behind. They thought it was the same one, but we knew better. Sometimes the one tailing behind was the mother, sometimes it was one of the fathers. Always though, the three were in love.

The squabs became more mourning doves, and some kept to our valleys and our peaks. Others flew away. Others met less beautiful, yet still necessary ends (at least necessary for the hawk or the eagle or the falcon). Nature has a way of defying the practical definitions that people try to draw around it with their fierce geometry, so often they mold it to what fits their narrow angles of understanding, but nature is not within the understanding of people.

It exists beyond the boundary of people. It

encompasses them, will survive them, and came before them. Nature will consume them and will allow them the grace to live. Without nature, people alone have no family, and yet people try to confine it to their own laws of justice, of what is pure and correct.

Nothing in nature is pure; nothing in nature is correct.

Our hill, which is us is not only a home to demise and destruction and death and loss. We are a home to love and birth and friendship. We are a home to the lonely, who are then found. Poems have been written on our hills, bears sleep deep within our gullies and caves that people have not found useful. Deer play and rut.

This all still occurs. How can we be dying, we a force of nature, a primordial example and testament to its permanence and process? There is so much life left yet to be seen and experienced. It is you, Death of Mountains, that grants people the justice of power over that existence.

It is you, Death of Mountains, who offers people the tools to which they have no right.

SUMMIT'S REFRAIN: PLUNDERED MOUNTAIN

On our hill, which is us, Death of Mountains listens to our story as the moon begins to hide her magnificence behind the other (far larger) hills and mountains within our view. Our sisters' trees are far taller and their peaks far more rocky and more impressive than our own have ever been. We are but a middling, small hill, yet we have always been content with this. There is no need to be grand, only to be. Death of Mountains stands looking at the moon as she descends; they do this for some time, as if thinking, before they turn again to face our peak.

"People have a lot of power," they say. "Too much, really."

"This is what we say also."

"People are the cause of all the deaths I was late for. I mean, really, thinking about it, they make the Death of Rivers extremely angry all the time. The Death of Insects will not stop complaining about them. Death of Pets is incensed about them constantly, more constantly than constantly." The Death of Mountains shudders, once again sending coal dust from both their mouth and their cloak falling to my frost-rimed hill. "What if I could convince the Death of People to, you know, just get rid of people."

"That is a little too harsh a solution, don't you think?"

We have seen much joy from the lives of ants and stars and rivers, we have seen just as much from the lives of people themselves. We have seen just as much wonder and wondered just as much about their lives. The poet, the person driving the car, the man whose shoulders held back the morning, and others we have not mentioned. All of them have brought us so much joy over the time we remained here. Joy, and pain yes, but overwhelmingly joy.

Ridding one entire set of beings to save others is never a solution.

"It's a bet worth making," Death of Mountains says.

"And would we still die, before the bet was made? You have come here to do a job, Death of Mountains. We would hate for you to fail in this job, and then render your entire position forfeit over not completing it, simply for a useless vendetta. For a blithe hope."

They smile, the Death of Mountains, and the smile opens fissures in their skull.

"Why not invite Death of People here for the whole shebang? I mean, when you die, people will die, he'll have to be here anyway."

"So, we are to die, there is no route around the event."

"Maybe. Maybe not, I haven't decided yet."

The staff they hold is heavy in their grip, their fingers fracking as they hold it, as it is staked firm in the ground. As if they were concerned about falling onto that great road in a whorl of smoke and fury. But we are only concerned with their last statement: they have not decided yet whether we are to die. There is yet a chance for us to remain as us, for one middling hill in the Appalachians to have conquered Death.

What a glorious thing.

THE DEATH OF PEOPLE'S SECOND STORY

GOT A STORY FOR YOU, and it goes like this: Creativity is not in my purview. Like at all. We don't have a Death of Machines. Maybe we should; maybe we should talk to Below about making one. I mean, machines just sometimes kaput at super inconvenient times, which is great! Computers, phones, cars, gas pumps, and not only those. I mean even guns do, as well as bombs and tanks! Everything ever made is super unreliable. Even Deaths, even me.

Today I'm at a park, as well as a highway, as well as a synagogue. We get it, everyone gets it. Every day, I am in millions of places at once, helping people move along. People who die in their sleep, people who die in schools, in car crashes. People who die quietly (the minority), and people who die scared (most people).

Then there are days like today where I am at another war crime while also at a mall while *also* at all the other places, and all I want to do is sit in this park and watch people do things that people do: swing on swings, laugh, hold hands maybe. I don't know, I could have a coffee in one hand and a donut in the other, watching people be people.

But I can't.

Instead, I gotta usher people onwards to the next life (knowing where isn't in my purview, either). I'm here, minding my own business at this park. The caution tape is surrounding me and there's blankets over bodies as if they're going to get cold. Radio chatter comes over everything garbled, and I am nearing the last blanket when someone walks up and takes my hand.

My first thought is, this isn't good.

My second thought is, no, it's worse. The hand belongs to a young woman and she's looking at me, asking where her boyfriend is. I just sent him off a moment ago, and now it's her turn. My hand is as cold and weirder than hers. Was created to look like a messed-up sort of human being (like all the Deaths but at least I dress to blend in, sorta), and I smile at her. She smiles back.

"Hey," I say. "I know where he is. Just breathe six times and you'll find him."

"Six times?"

"Yeah," I say. "Yeah, just six. And then you'll be out of here. Okay?"

She nods and takes my instruction. Takes one deep breath, then two.

By the third one? She's gone.

All this is to say that when I finally get Death of Mountains' message to come to the middle of fucking nowhere West Virginia, U.S.A.? I took it. Of course, I took it. There's a lot of rules to being Death of People, and one of them is that I have to be everywhere at once. So, gallivanting off to West Virginia is part of being everywhere at once, and Below can chew me out later about it. Anyway, I'm their favorite, their absolute Employee of the Month, every month (Employee of Eternity, really). There's nothing they can do to stop me.

Normally, when I get a message from another Death it's: *Please make all of this stop. Please make people stop.* It's like seeing politicians on the news stations: thoughts and prayers, looking to their gods, wishing tragedy away. It's impossible. I can't make people stop, any more than I can stop the killing from happening.

Death of Mountains had a different message this time, and it said: *Hey, got a proposition for you, come find me.* Which is super easy to do, because Death of Mountains smells like half volcano and half coal mine, and I am well acquainted with both (because people have died in each way too many times). So, when I went to find them, they were standing on a mountain that looked standard, to me. A small hill in the Appalachians that looked like every other small hill in the Appalachians (but I'm no geologist).

Some of the hill had been gored out for coal mining, some of it sliced away to make a highway. Seen this all the time on my trips here. This is what people do, they renovate stuff to look like them, and they die in the process. They kill in the process. They gloat in the process. It's a whole thing.

Not a fan of that ingenuity, either.

People's need to make not only their kids look like them, and their companies look like them, and their deeds look like them, but the land too. It's always the worst ones that do this, the ones that I end up having zero remorse for and who end up begging me to let them live a little while longer to finish their *legacy*. Their legacy never has to deal with their children, or what they mean to give back to the world. It always has to deal with what they need to do so they can carve their name in history.

History remembers maybe only a handful of names. One of my handfuls. And my hands can hold two millennia of names and has. Most people's names aren't remembered kindly, I'll just say. People who die wanting to carve their names in history are always the ones who get the super angry write-ups in books later.

Anyway, Death of Mountains is waiting for me a couple of hours before dawn. Time means nothing to most Deaths, but it means everything to me, because it means a lot to people. It's basically a construct that humanity pays a lot of attention to (and animals, but they don't track it by the second like people do). So, it's a couple of hours before dawn, which means the people are probably coming back to this active coal mine which smells like pending death. Stinks of it, even.

Death of Mountains is sitting on a log like they're exhausted. The mountain is being a mountain, and she introduces herself to me as Plundered Mountain. I introduce myself as Death of People, which makes her laugh. It sounds like a rock tumbler. The movement of her earth upsets the frost rime over her dwindling moss, turning it to water. Basically, making it rain on my wide brimmed hat and my faded blazer. So faded that it looks dusty. It's supposed to be black, now it looks a mess.

The Death of Mountains commits to the bit of being a Death. Most of them do, but I gotta pass among people. So, I just look like I'm dying, in all places at once, all the time. I reach a pale (almost blue) hand up to the brim of my hat to flick the water off when the mountain answers in her own voice.

"We know you, Death of People. We've seen you often, in all different ways of dress, in all different eras of your being. The last time we saw you in this way, you came for one of the workers in our deep and diving cave. You were the same: in the coat and hat. Your shoes were different, fit for such a place. But you were the same, your step making no weight upon the roots of the plants that find solace here."

I can't help but smile at this mountain, and Death of Mountains, too. "Well, nice to meet 'cha, Plundered Mountain. And hear your voice. Now we're acquainted."

"Friends, we are friends. As the Death of Mountains and I are friends."

They sigh, Death of Mountains does, and their face away with a pissed off grumble. They're always pissed, always grumbling. Stubborn as a mountain themselves, this one. We all take on our guises, as much as the Deaths say they don't. But we gotta. It's our job.

"Now you've gone and made it personal, dammit," they say.

"Personal, and harder." I lean my elbow on their staff, to make things even more personal. "So, what's this bargain, anyway. I'm very busy."

The Death of Mountains looks up at me, their face erupting into a grin. "This is something I think you'll like. Can you talk to Below? They love you down there, I think you can get this done. I think only you can get this done."

"Oh yeah?"

"Oh yeah."

"And what is it *only I* can get done? Spit it out." I ask.

My grin is as wide as theirs, but my lean gets harder on their staff. So much so that Death of Mountains has to stand and flick me away like the nuisance I am. Their annoyance and their confidence work in tandem, like a volcano. It's a hobby of mine to get to the root of entities and people, and Death of Mountains is extremely easy to get to the core of. I mean, all they are is core.

When they've composed themselves as much as they can (which isn't much), they say. "I need you to get them to make another one. Another one of us, you know, another Death."

Boring, so boring. I get asked this a lot. It never works. So many of the Deaths want me, the Employee of Eternity to get them an assistant death. Someone who can help them do their jobs so that they (the main Death) can go on vacation or like have a cocktail or take a nap or something. I do what they ask because it makes me, Death of People, look better. Cause if I'm not the one asking for an assistant—me, who is the busiest of all the Deaths (after Death of Trees stopped being busier about 50 years ago)—isn't asking for an assistant, well? It looks bad for everyone else.

"I dunno," I say, "that's kind of a big ask. Never

worked before, and it's gonna earn you a promotion. Is that what you want?"

Death of Mountains though seems to have a better idea, not the one I thought. They lean in, and say, "Not the usual thing, my guy. I need you to ask them to create a Death of Machines."

The mountain stills, Death of Mountains stills, and my jaw drops. I gotta say, for the first time in a long time (a century), I am intrigued. Intrigued and interested. More than interested, I am really, really interested.

SUMMIT'S REFRAIN: PLUNDERED MOUNTAIN

On our hill, which is us, we watch Death of People's face swirl like a storm when the Death of Mountains said their piece to him. Of which Death they wanted created. We had our own dislike of machines, the smoke they billowed up that choked our trees and cut them down and killed our deer and scared our bears and so much else.

We do not like machines.

They need to die as much as mountains do, as people do, as bears and plants and insects do. When Death of People's face finally settles on an expression (it goes through several: surprise, delight, doubt) it settles on thoughtful consideration when he turns to the Death of Mountains. He takes his hat off, holding it in both hands like someone finding something concerning among the weeds.

"Now that? That is a fucking great idea."

"So, you'll do it then? Do you think you can, even?"

Death of People turns his hat twice in his hands. Twice and then half again. "Oh, hell yeah, I'll do it. I'll do it and I'll lobby to be the guy to take it on. I hate machines more than I hate people's ingenuity."

We feel the first signs of dawn crest over the furthest of our sisters' peaks. We know it, all mountains speak to one another, all connected ones, and we Appalachians are connected. The horizon is far off, but our sister can feel it. We know our time is near. We are to die, unless Death of People can succeed with his bargain.

"There is not much time, Death of Mountains. Morning is close, and the miners will return soon."

They turn to Death of People. "You heard her, get going."

"You're too soft on those you kill."

His hat on, Death of People turns and walks away down my narrow paths, pulling at tree branches and continuing to be excellent at being him: a problem. Death of People always was, from what we remember, and when he is gone, when we can feel him gone, the Death of Mountains turns to me.

"I don't hate anything about you Plundered Mountain."

"We know you do not, you cannot hate a thing to be so patient with it."

There is another pause, yet we are impatient. The decision is not yet made on whether we will we die, or whether we will we not die. Our life is in the hands of an entity we do not trust, in the hands of two entities whose entire job it is to ensure that lives end, and we have nothing but time. Time, another entity which has been nothing but patient with us.

"Death of Mountains, we would have another game of questions."

"It's not a game, it's a conversation."

"Still yet, we would have it," we say, sensing their irritation.

Perhaps they, too, are impatient with their lack of success with us. Their lack of success with so much. Perhaps we stand as a testament to their failures, a permanent monument to their inability to succeed. This must upset them, but our life is not a game nor is it a goal, much like the game of questions is not a game. Nor is it a goal.

"Fine, ask away," they say, finally.

And we begin.

THE SECOND GAME OF QUESTIONS

Plundered Mountain: "Did you hate any of the mountains you killed? Ever?"

Death of Mountains: "No. Some of us Deaths aren't as burdened as Death of People is. Or Death of Pets. Or Death of Trees was, a while back. The less busy entities like me don't have to speak to a mountain that has eyes and expressions and a mouth. Or was so busy for so long that we lose empathy for everything under our care. You don't have a face with expressions, and when you die, I just leave and never return to the site again. Mountains don't die in such numbers that I'm overwhelmed by how busy I am. But like every death of every living thing on this earth, each mountain's death is unique. Each of you fall in different patterns and leave different scars of devastation on the ground. Sure, you all wreak havoc and cause catastrophes by dying. It's amazing, really, how dramatic you are in both living and dying. But Death of People? He has to see peoples' expressions, and when they're dead in millions of places at once. Sometimes people die peacefully, most don't though, I bet. And a lot of people's deaths are the same, over and over. The people, though, are unique, and he has had to deal with that since people were invented. So, I guess that took a lot out of him. He's good at his job, and that can sometimes be a problem."

Plundered Mountain: "Yet he cannot simply stop doing his job?"

Death of Mountains: "No way. If people stopped dying, the whole world would freak out. Can you imagine if the worst people never stopped dying and the people they hated never stopped dying either? It's not like people would stop *being*, they would just stop *dying*. People can be inventive about hurting each other, and things, and other living things. If people stopped dying, they'd find inventive ways of hurting one another, and one another's things. Basically, the worst people would become worser and the people living terrible lives would keep living even more terrible lives. The entire land itself—like you—would suffer for their immortality. I would suffer. Better to make Death of People suffer, cause he's insufferable."

Plundered Mountain: "And creating a Death of Machines would change this?"

Death of Mountains: "I think it would change everything."

Death of Mountains: "Can you remember a time before machines?"

Plundered Mountain: "We struggle to. Our memory spans time before people counted time the way they do now. We remember so much, but so much of us has been gored away and cut away, and memories can get lost in so much hurt and pain. Just as so much of us has been lost and mowed away, so much destroyed and chased and cut down, so too has happened to our memory. For so many passages of the snow and sun and seasons, for so many of these times, so much of all of this was done by machines. Machines with blades are so cruel and unfeeling in the way they hurt us, the way they hurt anything. There is no thought to how they do it, the machines simply do as they are told. We struggle to remember a time before machines, as people do. Before there were machines to gore out what we kept inside us, our precious things, our metals and our fuel and our food, many people died. Yet is that better? What is better to keep ourselves precious, or for people to fall to their own curiosity? We are unsure. This is what we know: we enjoyed being a whole Plundered Mountain before we became plundered, and we know that machines did the bulk of this: cut us in two, carved our paths, delved deep down inside us and continue to do so. But we also know it was the people who did this. But there is already a Death of People, and we know that Death of People cannot stop the machines."

Death of Mountains: "So do you believe a Death of Machines is necessary?"

Plundered Mountain: "We believe that death of all things is necessary. Including mountains; including machines.

SUMMIT'S REFRAIN: PLUNDERED MOUNTAIN

On our hill, which is us, we answer the second of Death of Mountains' game of questions, and they are pleased. They turn from their log and face down the gorge at the coming dawn, diffused as it is by the clouds that have come in the night. The sky is heavy with the idea of rain, but not the threat of it. It simply thinks of raining. Which the sky often does this early in spring.

On our hill, which always has been us, the sky once did not only think of raining, but it also simply rained more often when it wanted to. Considering rain never occurred to it for too overlong. Perhaps it would consider rain in the heat of the summer, making the animals and the people dismal. Otherwise, the sky rained on schedule. The seasons at that time were evenly dealt out like a picnic upon my summits. Yet the summers bled into the autumns which never ended as the stars and birdsong disappeared. The seasons and the sky became mercurial. The sky thinks of raining and does not. Or does not think of raining and does. The trees wither in the dry soil and then are overcome by deluge and fall.

The sky is as unpredictable as all things, including people, including death. Including the Deaths. One of which is now standing overlooking my gorge, high above the deep and diving cave. There is a long road which leads up what used to be a part of me to this cave mouth. To the entrance where on our hill, which was still then us, the man whose shoulders held back the morning walked out cradling Sunshine in his hands.

Upon this road now, we can hear the familiar sound of a truck. We know it is driven by a serious woman of serious means. She is wide of hip and wide of shoulder. We know her voice sounds like smoke and always of laughter. We know her car sounds like her laugh: like coughing. Death of Mountains hears this too.

"The people are coming to kill you soon," they say.

"We know."

"Maybe it's preventable, maybe." Death of Mountains turns their head. They are annoyed, their entire posture says so, their shoulders raised to the jutting eddies of their jawline, their stone skull face fracked into an expression of incredulity. "I am Death of Mountains, so it is me who says when you go."

"But the people do as they wish, we have heard you say over and over. They could kill me without your ability to interfere."

"Not while I stand here, they can't."

They say this with such finality and conviction, but their posture fails to convince us. This is evident in the way they slowly turn away from the gorge with one glance at it. One glance, as if daring the very land to defy them.

"I got another story for you," they say, standing still in that uncertain posture. Their staff staked in the ground to keep them upright. "One more story, and then we'll know."

"One more," we say. "This is your promise."

"One more."

And they begin.

THE DEATH OF MOUNTAINS' THIRD STORY

For the sake of this story, I am, all told, not very good at my job.

Death of People is better at my job than me. This is my current worry as dawn creeps up and through your mining gorge and drifts along a highway that splits you in half. As vehicles meander and pass on the highway, they create a new atmosphere that I had not yet felt along your landscape, or in your demeanor. When the traffic begins, I am watching your tension rise. First, I feel it in the core of you, since I, myself, am basically a core. I feel the mine groan and the gasses shift, I feel you crawl a little closer to death. This all moves up from the core of you to the roots of the trees, that I can see. They shift and sway, and even the moss under my feet can feel it, but it reacts differently: its small flowers open and yawn their petals toward the grey sky.

Rabbits exit their warrens to eat these flowers, and the vehicles provide a rushing, rattling cacophony that mimics the very reason I am here. The machines which have bonded us—you and I—have risen for the day. The people that control them are awake and ready to do whatever it is people do in their machines, with their machines, to their machines.

That's when I realize, I am so incredibly out of time.

The truck that arrived in the gorge is red with peeling paint and has the back bed covered in a tarp held down by rubber cords. The woman who exited lights a cigarette; she covers her eyes to look at the sky. She must assume it is going to rain (a safe assumption), so she reaches back into the truck and pulls out a baseball cap before adjusting her coveralls to smoke and stands, waiting. As you and I are waiting. We are all waiting.

I note the details about her: the roughness of her hair, from too long in the mines, the same of her fingernails. How she stands with the confidence of you, never to be toppled over. She is a woman who has seen too much, experienced too much, and Hell will have to come knocking before she allows it to happen again.

Her hips are wide as her shoulders, a mountain of a woman. More reminders of you.

Another vehicle parks beside her and she smiles. It is the softest I have seen her yet, and I turn away. I get really attached to things: mountains, people, the idea of living. This, all told, is why I am bad at my job. When an entity must see to the deaths of things so permanent as a mountain, they get permanent, too, I guess. Permanent in my feelings, in my memories, in my conversations. Like I said, attached.

A mountain is also an entity, as you said, as you carry so much on your shoulders. Like we Deaths carry so much on our shoulders. Honestly, I'd never thought about that, how I carry so much around. As not only do I witness and carry the mountains to their deaths, but I also carry all those upon them to this too: the trees, the rabbits, the bears, the deer, all their roots and homes and plants.

It is a lot to care about, and I care way too much.

Down in the gorge, the woman leans on her truck as she speaks to a man with a grey beard gone black in places from coal dust that will never quite wash out. He has a face that would be younger had it not given up like he's given up on trying to find better work. Life here is hard, and it's harder on people.

As I watch them, I understand why Death of People is so upset all the time.

Is it truly their fault, these two individuals, that you have to die? Not really, not at all really. What they're trying to do is feed themselves, maybe they have families, maybe they have lovers, and those lovers have a family. I can't even guess how people live their lives. This man and this woman seem cordial to one another, even more cordial than cordial. Friendlier than friendly. The man laughs and takes a cigarette from the woman, she lights it, he holds her hand while she does.

Oh, they like-like one another. Oh no.

These people are not at fault for killing you, especially not these two. I'm deciding that right now. I'm extending that offer also to the other five that drive up and exit their vehicles in similar dress and converse laughing and joking. They turn and watch the mine's closed doors with suspicion, as if they also know that there's something wrong with the place as I do. Like you do, too.

It's not their fault. They're just trying to be happy, probably failing at it most of the time, but hanging on to those bright spots of every few or several days to keep going. Coming to work and going back to work. And for what? To have it all end today.

We can't let this happen; I won't let this happen.
Okay that was it, that was the story.

SUMMIT'S REFRAIN: PLUNDERED MOUNTAIN

ON OUR HILL, WHICH IS US, it is morning.

All mornings are abrupt, yet no morning is as abrupt as the morning one is to die. The dawn leaves swiftly and is accompanied by the sky turning from grey to blue with the din of laughter and highway traffic. They have arrived, the people: the commuters, the miners, the hikers. All of them here to live and to die in my own destruction.

Death of Mountains' posture seems smaller as the morning crawls on. After their story (which was not a story but more of a soliloquy) echoes in my head. They had much to say, and so much of it still tenses in my core and sets all of me—and all upon me and around me—to an unease they cannot understand. Even Death of Mountains finds themselves in a state of emotional disarray.

"We have to stop this," they say.

"We cannot stop this, Death of Mountains. You are a Death, you are the one who is able, not me. We cannot stop ourselves from doing what it is we are meant to do."

"I gotta be honest with you, Plundered Mountain. I'm not super confident about this."

Our sigh is so great that it exits a groan from the deep and diving shaft and causes trees to tumble downward from the cliff that divides us in two. The trees fall branches over roots, over my cliff and onto the highway, shattering there. We hear a a squeal of tires and the agonizing creak and crash of metal. Two sets: they impact, loudly. This, we know, is our fault; this, we know, is something we have done. Normally, we would be upset that we have done such things. Or when such things happen without our interference. Yet today, the day of our own death, we are selfish. We want to only mourn ourselves.

And we do, for a moment or two, until the Death of People arrives.

He arrives in a flurry of activity and business, like people themselves do. Always in a hurry to do something (or nothing at all). People have purpose always, or nearly always, and Death of People is no different in that regard. He walks immediately to my cliff and points down to the highway. The gesture is accusatory, as is his tone when he speaks. The entire flash of moments from his arrival to the time he speaks takes enough time for the birds to notice and take flight.

Hardly any time at all. Death of People is swift. He would have to be, to be himself.

"Look what you did," he says. "Now I gotta clean this shit up, fuck's sake. Was going to give you some news, but first I gotta clean up this mess. Will tell you two all about it when I get back."

He disappears to the road as if he was never here, leaving behind him the nervous energy of a thousand people in his wake. Our impatience grows, the bear who woke this morning from her hibernation is even more agitated, the deer are skittish, and the rabbits too. They sense us as we are—all are connected. The workers too sense it: they have not yet entered our deep and diving cave. The door not yet unlocked, the man with the keys also hesitates.

All know something is wrong.

Death of People must think himself above all things, like some people tend to. The hubris of people (and Death of People) to think they alone can save a mountain, to think he can save me from Death of Mountains, from people themselves. It is true that he has been tasked with this, but it was the idea of Death of Mountains and ourselves which set him on this task, not his own. Like people themselves, he took this idea from the very world around him and molded it into his own image.

Yet the Death of Mountains is of another mind. As the Death of People disappears to the road, the Death of Mountains turns to face our peak, their expression hopeful. They approach closer than they ever have before, their voice rumbling in a whisper that shakes our entire core. They lean close, this is only for us to hear: them and us.

"Hopefully, just hopefully, he has a plan."

"What of you, Death of Mountains, do you have a plan?"

They step back, looking confused. "Me? Never."

People normally have plans, even when they do not, others surrounding them have one: there are plans that overlap plans that overlap plans. The Death of People would be no different. We suspect that when he took the Death of Mountains' request to Below, he had his own plan that differed from Death of Mountains' request, that differed from our desires.

But we do not know what that was.

THE DEATH OF PEOPLE'S THIRD STORY

Got a story for you, and it goes like this: no amount of being the best employee ever in the history of eternity could get a Death of Machines assigned. Not by the operators of Below, not by me, not even by being a petulant entity and whining. Because apparently all things that die have to have a soul, and according to the operators of Below, machines don't have souls. This is total bullshit, machines not having souls. They are just as cantankerous and opinionated as the best and the worst people on earth (machines are more like cats than people, really). I kind of lost my cool, and whined at them saying, *Okay but, it's not people doing the killing right now, the machines are doing most of it.*

Then an operator said, *That sounds like a you problem, Death of People.*

Another operator said, *People control machines, machines do not act as an entity unto themselves. So, your argument is forfeit. Meeting adjourned, don't you think?*

A *me* problem. Right. Okay, you can say that people kill people, but without machines, I really think that the people killing people would go down like a lot. It doesn't take a lot of thinking to realize that it's machines that do a really good job of doing the actual job. So, if we can, you know, take the machines out of the equation sometimes (most of the time)? It'll lower the killing a bunch.

It's not like I have a choice on what people do with their actual lived lives, I only make sure their soul gets sent to the proper place (no I don't know where, that's not in my purview, either). Doing that was a lot easier when machines that kill weren't so portable or had so many easily pressable buttons. Or were so easy for people to get their hands on.

The fact that the operators would even pretend that the machines aren't doing the killing is insulting. I was insulted on my way out of Below (down the hall to the left, through the double doors, to the elevator that takes way too long to arrive and always sounds like it's about to fall apart). Was still insulted while I waited for the elevator when this one operator joined me at the elevator doors. They're a squirrelly one, this guy. Never say much at meetings, always look at everyone else like their ideas are too wacky for Wackyworld. Never know if they're a good operator or a bad operator. Operators with ideas are freaky. This operator stood next to me for a long time, not saying anything, rocking back and forth from heel to toe. Then, after about three minutes, they said, *I have a solution to your problem.*

Unexpected but overjoyed, I looked down at them and said, *Oh yeah?*

They entered the elevator with me, and we took the long way up (the route that goes to all the floors). The operator stalled six floors before they spoke, probably making sure no one else was getting on. Then when they talked, they didn't shut up, and what they said hardly made sense.

First, they talked about how Deaths have *will*, and how having that will is *better* than having a soul. Which I took to mean that Deaths can't die. Then they went on about how earlier is better than on time is better than late. Which I took to mean duh. After that they talked about how if a Death arrives early, dying can be avoided. Then they winked super hard like a cartoon character, and that's when I got really annoyed.

I said, *What the fuck are you talking about?*

They said, *All a Death needs to do is arrive before the event of the dying, killing, massacre, so on. Then the Death has to will the machine doing the killing to give up: malfunction, turn off, stop working, jam, et cetera. Whatever it is the pertinent machine needs to do to stop working. Do you follow?*

So, I said, *And any Death can do this?*

The operator said, *Yes, as they arrive before the actual dying occurs. And, as long as the dying would be caused by machine. Machine and a person, or machine and another machine, or a machine and something else. A machine plus, as it were.*

The operator went on to say that the machine doesn't die, because machines don't really die. That's whatever the word anthropomorphizing would be for machines. The arriving Death would be causing a convenient oopsie-doodle, thus preventing one death or many deaths. This operator was very excited about this idea of theirs.

And I said, *Don't get me wrong, but isn't this kind of out of our purview?*

And they said, *You wanted less work, Death of People. This is how you get it, sort of. But I didn't say anything, and I was never here. I really don't want to get promoted.*

They pushed a button on the elevator and walked off at the cafeteria floor. I rode the elevator all the way up to Plundered Mountain, where I'm now standing with the *Sort Of* haunting me as I stand on the highway over a car wreck with absolutely zero casualties.

The cars saved these people's lives, the cars, the airbags, everything. The ambulances, the machines in the ambulances all beeping and booping and dripping and all of that. Guess I never considered that, how machines can work both ways: saving and killing. When I only see them go one way forever and ever and ever, I never get to see them do any good.

I decide not to tell Plundered Mountain or Death of Mountains about the good machines, as I have a pitch to make. The 'machines might be good actually' turn of events might send Death of Mountains into a moral quandary and they'd be sitting on that log for the rest of time. Well, the rest of time until they get promoted.

Perspective, I guess, is all the rage.

SUMMIT'S REFRAIN: PLUNDERED MOUNTAIN

On our hill, which is us, Death of People's joyful mood strikes us as an ill omen.

We are struck with worry over his smiling and carrying on, Death of Mountains as well. They turn from where they have been standing, watching the arrival of the people in the gorge and their conversations and rumble their discontent. We have heard similar sounds of discontent from people themselves, but it did not sound so low or cause us to rumble. The people who remain standing in the gorge start speaking louder as our sympathetic discontent causes small stones to fall from our hillside.

Death of People's mood is unmistakable. He strides with a weightless step across my summit toward the Death of Mountains and claps them on their craggy shoulder with so human a gesture that it is difficult for us to forget that he is not human.

And he says, "I got a solution to your problem. Well, to all our problems. To your problem, too, Plundered Mountain. I think we can fix all these issues right here, right now, tout suite. All we gotta do is just exercise our extreme will that we have as Deaths. You got that still, right? Extreme will? Death of Mountains? You haven't lost that along with everything else?"

Death of Mountains grinds their stone teeth. "I kill mountains; of course, I have will."

Death of People claps his hands together, his excitement so palpable that rabbits turn their ears back and deer retreat slowly, one hoof behind the other, in the wake of his presence. They can sense his overwhelming humanity even though he is not here for them. His smile grows too wide for his too long a face as he turns his face down to the deep and diving cave that plummets to my core.

"Then we go down there, I'll explain as we go."

"You're terrible at explaining things on the fly," Death of Mountains says. "Let me know the plan now or things will get muddy and so will Plundered Mountain."

And so, Death of People explains.

He explains that the machines work at the will of the people, and it is the people that cause the machines to work. Yet even Death of People cannot destroy a person's will; only a person can destroy the will of an individual (or their own will). Yet a machine itself has no will: *Not yet, anyway. So that's where we come in: We have will, the machine doesn't.* He continues to say that all Deaths have a will that can prevent a death before it occurs.

"Now, normally, this is a big no-no," he says.

"Right, everyone knows that."

Death of People goes on to say that yet for entities without souls, such as machines, ending their will to do anything, such as work or function or go forward or up and down? It is apparently not entirely against the rules. So, to create a death of machines, which is not allowed—as machines do not have souls—all a Death has to do is simply—

"But I'm always late to everything," Death of Mountains says.

"Well, maybe this'll motivate you to change that behavior, right, buddy?"

Death of People claps them on their craggy shoulder once more, sending a brush of coal dust to the moss yet again. Death of Mountains looks down to the gorge below, to the people filing for the elevator to take them deep and diving into our plunging depths, and perhaps today to their death and mine.

That is, if these two Deaths cannot will the task in front of them to be.

THE PLUNDERED MOUNTAIN'S THIRD STORY

On our hill, which is us, we feel all that goes on within us or upon us. As a mountain, we feel and know all things that touch us: all roots, all hands, all embers. All things left behind. We have been burned and reborn. We have been cried upon and died upon. We have been cleaved in and gored out. Birthed upon and coupled upon. Time has told its tale upon us over and over and remade us again and again.

We remember a time when insect calls were so plentiful that we could not name them all; their songs of mating were so loud at night that they kept the similar songs of animals company. Now, we are not so alive in the night. Now we are not so alive.

When the Deaths leave our summit, we allow ourselves to worry less. The deed will either be done or undone. We feel as if both coalesce in the elevator to the deep and diving cave. They arrive beside the people, the people who work the mine. The people become nearly as uneasy as I have been with Death of Mountains on my shoulder. There is a sense when a Death is nearby (whether that Death is for us or not), we feel ourselves dying all around us and within us. We become wholly aware of how alive we are and how that sense of living is finite. We would imagine a person would feel their body decay as we have felt ourselves decay all those times.

That sense has been more acute since Death of Mountains arrived. With Death of People at the workers' shoulders, their sense of fear must be as high as mine. Or maybe they cannot name their feeling, as we could not name it for so long. Perhaps they pass it off with jokes and games, as we did for so long. We can only hope that the fear will pass, and the people, and we, will live to see the moon in the sky this night and many more nights to come.

As Death of Mountains visited this past night, we considered our long existence: how much joy we had, how much pain, how much we had seen. There was much more joy than pain, we would like to say. But a mountain is meant to hold up the hopes of the world. We are monuments, testaments to permanence, no matter how people might change us and alter us to fit their convenience. No matter how they take from us how we fit, how we provide them convenience.

Yet, in the abundance of joy we have experienced in our lifetime, we are still in pain. Not only from the place where the Deaths and the people are going, but from the road where people are now stopped in their vehicles as the tree that fell from one of my hills is cleared. From the deaths we witnessed over our dying months and years, and the deaths of those we witnessed that were unjust, or painful to witness.

While we never wanted to die, has our decision changed? As the chainsaws sing and the elevator groans and the hawks cry, we wonder: is this the symphony we want to hear for another lifetime? Would we choose to exist more only to be scraped from within and cleaved once again, and to have people kill upon us and burn us more, and more, and more.

And we say, *Yes. Yes, we would.*

For all pain there is joy that outweighs pain's measure. There are mourning doves and black bears and the little girl who learned to tie her shoes upon our trail. There are soft dawns and brilliant moon rises and the stars that we can still yet see. Perhaps the stars will return one day, and we will want to be here when they return.

We feel when the elevator reaches its destination.

We feel these things. The elevator and the people: the people's lack of joy and their worry as well as their conviction; the elevator's scrape along our walls as its cables and metal safely deliver the people to the mine. The people do not want to begin work. They walk slowly out from the metal doors, slower than they entered them. The depths make them do this, the dark makes them do this, the Deaths make them do this. The toil as well. As it does, we feel them all walk down the narrow pathways; we feel them walk toward the machines.

We have always felt the machines. We have felt them in their idleness, the potential of their pain and hurt, a constant reminder of what they could do. The threat of them, the purpose of them. All things people have created have purpose: that is why people create, to make something to perform or proliferate said purpose. Even when not wielded by a person, the machines will lay idle upon my floor, safely locked away, or elsewhere. They are heavy with the need to be the tool of which they are.

We have always felt the machines.

They rumble and ache as they work against us. They pierce, and they scrape. They dive, and they delve, bore and cut. The machines in use have a far more malevolent and purposeful feeling than a machine in idleness. As so is a person.

Yet today, their presence is… is absent. Their purpose missing. The people's confusion is evident in their shuffled step along the mine's floor. Deep and deeper underground. Some of them bang the machines against the walls of my deep and diving depths. Some of them hit the machines themselves, the sound echoing along my caverns, ringing with no answer. We feel the people's fury at all the machines, simply ceasing to be machines. But is what they feel fury? Is it confusion?

Or is it simply joy?

The idea spreads quickly that nothing at all works, and that no work can be done. Not today, perhaps not for several days. The elevator yet works, so too do the lights and the communication devices. They speak to one another in the cave, I can feel the warmth of the wire connecting lantern to lantern as four people converse next to one of the lights, speaking quickly, but in low whispers.

It is a different two people who ride the elevator up as the others collect their calm with lively discussion and wonder. They weave a story out of magic, of how the machines suddenly died. How the mine must have killed them; how had they arrived earlier, the mine would have killed them, too. The two that arrive back at the surface gesture widely, speaking in loud voices as they wait. They wait while the sun rises higher in the sky the sun rises higher in the sky, until two more vehicles arrive, larger ones. More purposeful ones.

Two men climb out, one from each truck. They carry large bags, and larger amounts of determination.

Their stride to the elevator is heavy and would disturb us, does disturb us. For a small moment, we think that the Deaths' plans could be undone by two men and their own smaller machines.

Yet they cannot.

As the sun lowers in the sky all the people had descended to the mine that morning emerge from the depths. Many of them leave, some swiftly, some not so. Only the two who summoned the two determined men—and the determined men—remain. They talk until the sun begins to set. They continue talking. One of them throws their hat on the ground. One determined man picks it up and hands it to the hatless one. The hatless one turns around to his vehicle and drives away swiftly.

The determined men leave, and only one person remains. He stands staring at the mine and sighs, turning to walk slowly to his car. He whistles a song as he goes, it does not sound like Sunshine's song had. It does not sound like it could hold back the night, or roll in the morning; instead, this sound is sad, as if it would usher the night in. This man drives away slowly, stopping once. He forgets to turn on his headlights until he is on the road that cleaves us in two.

The Deaths do not return.

Death of People is said to be at millions of places at once, millions of millions. He is too busy to return to us to assure us that the will of Death had done its work on the machines. This is something we know. We had not been entirely certain of the power of will, or of the power of will of any Deaths, or death itself. We are a mountain, and our will is absolute, it stands above all, or above most, a testament to permanence and songs and fury. As for the reason Death of Mountains did not return to say goodbye? We assume they had their reasons, the first being they were likely late to work.

We will miss them, Death of Mountains. They were kind. We can only hope they offer similar kindness to all other mountains they leave in the wake of their coal dust cloak and stone staff. Perhaps they will allow other mountains the same decision to remain as they allowed us; perhaps they can less late and more early to stop the machines before they begin.

The very idea of the will of Deaths has us questioning our own will, as Plundered Mountain. The will of all mountains being absolute, yes. But what is it we want? What do we, Plundered Mountain, will and have willed into being? We suppose it comes back to what the poet had said: *Is it not in the nature of all shoulders to hold up the cares that weigh upon them?*

People, however, are the most difficult. Sometimes it is easy to see what they are thinking. Some people wear their dreams in their expressions, the way that they move, the light of their eyes. Others keep their thoughts hidden. We do not know why. We suspect that some of the people in the depths of us today will be happy, some will be sad, some will be hiding their thoughts for a long time.

As always, the curiosity of a mountain lasts as long as it needs to.

Which is to say that it will last as long as the result has been satisfied. Once we know what will happen to us, regarding the deep and diving depths, we will think about the people until there are no more people to think about. We think about the man whose shoulders held back the morning, and we wonder where he is now. He is probably long dead; his story happened a very long time ago. Before people arrived at our gorge in cars. When people would walk to our gorge carrying a very small amount of things.

We wonder about the poet who spoke on our mountain about shoulders and the nature of them. Where is he? We only saw him a few seasons ago. But how many seasons is a few to us, and are many to him? And we will think about the people who sat at our lowest point, deep and diving depths, spinning a story of confusion and wonder. How they must also be so curious about what had happened and why.

We will wonder about them until we cease to be, until all of it ceases to be.

EPILOGUE: THE DEATH OF MOUNTAINS' FOURTH STORY

For the sake of this story, it's early, way too early to kill anything worth killing. Dawn is barely an idea: the birds are still asleep, and this mountain refuses to talk to me until the workers have had their morning coffee. Once again, I'm waiting. Once again, I'm sitting on another log trying to kill a mountain that probably shouldn't even be on any sort of list. It's just my luck that if I can't be late, I am too early. If I am early, I should have been late. There's no pleasing anyone, much less a mountain, who's been on this earth longer than me, longer than anyone.

Maybe, one day, I'll figure out how to be more stubborn. Figure out how to do something else with my existence. Take up filing papers in the wrong order or making worse decisions that put everyone at a disadvantage. Think about getting a job putting the numbers in the wrong corner on filing forms or something. The real bureaucracy stuff that the Below really values. Something that keeps me employed but still on everyone's shitlist.

Life's too short to be good at my job. Permanence is way too long, and I realize now that I don't have the stomach for it. Death of People has the demeanor, the attitude, and the PTO to take the rest of eternity off, but he can't. Not ever. I don't have the stomach to be here forever, arguing with mountains, listening to Below.

So, while the mountain wakes up, I climb down (slowly, so slowly), work my way past the workers talking and enjoying their cup of coffee, and to their machines. And slowly, so slowly, I will the machines to be ex-machines. To break. To malfunction. To have a bad day.

Today is the day I stop being Death of Mountains.

Today is the day I become Bane of Machines.

ACKNOWLEDGMENTS

I never thought I'd write another book. The process after the publication of my first book was so fraught that I nearly quit writing entirely. So this book is entirely CJ Lavigne's fault. I have her to thank first for telling me that someone wanted more of my books *so much* that I felt compelled to write another. Also firstly, I have to thank Steve Berman at Lethe Press for seeing how wonderful this book is, and believing in it. Secondly, I want to thank everyone at the SFWA Writing Dates for convincing me that people actually wanted to read about Death of Mountains and Death of People and Plundered Mountain. Thank you. Every single one of you.

A book itself, is a mountain. An ecosystem. Both in the writing of it, and in its coming into being. I want to thank my best friend in the entire world, Josh Sabo, and my close friend Eric Christensen for being there for me while I whined about life and nearly fell apart several times over the last many years. Also my friends Steve and Matt for talking to me about books, writing, and the state of the world.

In the publishing arena, I want to thank Bogi Takács, Ada Hoffman, Karin Tidbeck, L.D. Lewis, Sarah Gailey, S.B.

Divya, Jon Lasser, Steen Comer, Maria Z. Medina, Spencer Ellsworth, Michelle Stewart, Marissa Lingen, Effie Seiberg, A.T. Greenblat, L.P. Kindred, Mina Li, Kate Heartfield, Lillian Boyd, Ai Jiang, Alex Shvartsman, Terra LeMay, Vajra Chandrasekera, Beth Dawkins, Denise Beuchler, and so many more I am probably forgetting.

Need to thank my incredible beta readers for *The Death of Mountains*, without whom I would have never gotten this far: Phoenix Alexander, P.A. Cornell, Rachel Ashcraft, and A.D. Sui.

My family is the reason that I am here and the reason I am curious about life. Without them, I would not have seen the world, and never have been curious about it. So many thanks to my mother, my step-father, my brother and sister, and my two step-brothers. My father, my step-mother, and their dogs. My extended step-family, and their dogs. Last but not least, my amazing nephew, whose love of life, the universe, and everything keeps me going.

Thank you all for reading. And thank you for continuing to tell the stories we need to live.

ABOUT THE AUTHOR

JORDAN KURELLA is a trans and disabled author who grew up all over the world, including Moscow and Manhattan, and in his past lives was a radio DJ, photographer, and social worker. Jordan's work can be found in *Reactor*, *Lightspeed*, and *Strange Horizons* magazines. His short fiction has been nominated for Best of the Net, long-listed for the British Science Fantasy Award, and short-listed for Best of the New Weird. Jordan's debut novella *I Never Liked You Anyway* was a Nebula Finalist and was long-listed for the BSFA award.